The Gryphon Press
—a voice for the voiceless—

This book is dedicated
to each person who rescues, fosters, adopts,
and takes responsible care of an animal.

To Emilie Buchwald, with respect and gratitude—k.d.

Text design by Karen Dugan
Text set in Warnock Pro by BookMobile Design and Publishing Services,
Minneapolis, Minnesota
Printed in Canada by Friesens Corporation

Library of Congress Control Number: 2008931119

ISBN: 978-0-940719-07-1

1 3 5 7 9 10 8 6 4 2

A portion of profits from this book will be
donated to shelters and animal rescue societies.

I am the voice of the voiceless:
Through me, the dumb shall speak;
Till the deaf world's ear be made to hear
The cry of the wordless weak.

—from a poem by Ella Wheeler Wilcox, early 20th-century poet

Ms. April & Ms. Mae

A fable

written and illustrated by
Karen Dugan

Ever since she was a girl,

Ms. April watched over her field and forest, pond and hill.

Everything she had, she shared with Ms. Mae, so alike, they could have been sisters. Whether they argued in birdese, murmured in buglish, whispered in reptili, or shouted in mammalian, they did their best always to end with a good laugh.

Every minute of their day
was filled with something to do:

Make seed and peanut butter sandwiches for the birds

Rescue caterpillars

Bury acorns and water baby trees

Watch ants

Climb rocks

Tickle the wind

Admire clouds

Compliment wildflowers

Sit for dragonflies

Take grassnaps

Make moss beds for toads

hmm hmm hmm
hmm hmm

Hum with bumblebees

But while Ms. April and Ms. Mae watched over
their field and forest, pond and hill,

to the north, skyscrapers tore apart gentle fields.

To the south, zooming highways smothered old dirt roads,

and to the east and west, ponds were drained and paved for malls, malls, and more malls.

Ms. Mae growled, but Ms. April spoke enough for two.
"Drat!" she said. "What the ding-dong is going on?"

Worst of all, when the new families arrived, the old families, the ones who crawled or flew or ran on more than two legs, were pushed aside. By ones and by twos (and if they were rabbits, by nines and by tens), they found Ms. April.

"Welcome, my dears," she said. "There is room for all.
And I promise, not one blade of grass will be pulled, or one leaf plucked,
as long as I can get around on my bony old legs."

And all was well—

until the morning Ms. April fell out of her favorite tree.

"Drat!" said Ms. April. "I won't go to the ding-dong hospital!
Who would take care of everyone?"

"Don't worry," said Ms. Mae. "It will be all right."

Every day, Ms. Mae watched over Ms. April, and every night, tip, tip, tap,

she watched over the field and forest, pond and hill.

One morning, Ms. April shivered with fever.
Ms. Mae knew how to brew a get-well tea, yet
the fever would take its time.

But time they did not have.

At that very moment, three men were delighted to hear Ms. April was nowhere to be seen. The idea of her sick, or even dead, made Misters Iddy, Oddic, and Dimm bounce on their toes, because they wanted every inch and acre of her field and forest, pond and hill.

Friends carried the bad news to Ms. Mae.

She trotted up to the attic.

    In a forest of old clothes, it was the quietest,

        although ("Achoo!") dustiest, place to think.

She thought:

If people knew Ms. April was sick,
they would take her away.

And, she thought:

Without Ms. April, everyone who crawls, or flies,
or runs on more than two legs will lose their homes.

Then, she thought:

No matter how many languages I speak, people listen only to people.

"Achoo!" Ms. Mae sneezed so hard, she began to fall against a tower of boxes. To save herself, she jumped.

In a dusty mirror, and with one more "Achoo!" Ms. Mae found her idea.

Next morning, the birds stopped in the middle of their song. The earth shook, trees shuddered, and dust billowed as machines roared up to Ms. April's stone wall.

"Get to work!" yelled the foreman.

Stones rolled and dirt flew until an ugly gash opened the way.

Ms. April, in her best hat, jumped from behind a bush and hopped here, there,

and down into a hole.

"We can't dig up the field if
Ms. April is down there," said the workmen.
So they left the field alone.

When they tried to chop down the forest, in the tallest pine swung Ms. April.

She jumped from tree tip to tree top until the workmen were dizzy.

"We can't cut down the forest
if Ms. April is up there," said the workmen.
So they left the forest alone.

When they tried to drain the pond, in the middle on a rock sat Ms. April.
She kicked and splashed the water until the workmen were all wet.

"We can't drain the pond if
Ms. April won't let us," said the workmen.
So they left the pond alone.

"Are you crazy?" asked Misters Iddy, Oddic, and Dimm.

"Dead old ladies don't jump down holes, or climb trees, or sit in ponds."

"*She* does," said the foreman, and he pointed toward the old house.

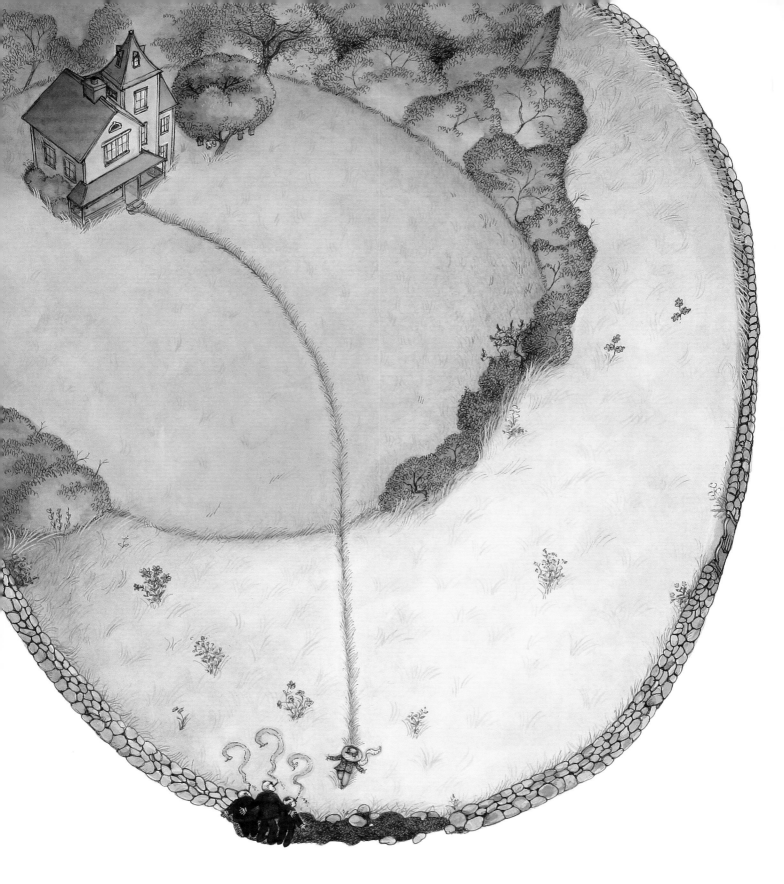

Over the porch rail and into the sunlight leapt a small figure.
The tall grass parted like a fine-tooth comb as the figure trotted, tip, tip, tap,
down to the broken wall. She walked like Ms. April, she looked like Ms. April,

and she sure sounded like Ms. April.

"Drat!" she said. "What the ding-dong are you boys doing to my beautiful wall?"

"Why, Ms. April!" said Misters Iddy, Oddic, and Dimm. "We thought you were dead!"

"Do I look dead? Do I even look tired?"
Through the heavy veil
on her best hat,
they saw only
her bright, bright eyes.

"Come with me," she said, and back up the hill she trotted, tip, tip, tap.
Misters Iddy, Oddic, and Dimm followed, clump, bump, thump.

"Tea, boys?" asked Ms. April.

The tea smelled like the sweet, watery wind after a summer rain.

"Cookies, boys?" asked Ms. April.

The spicy cookies bit the tips of their tongues and flaked like brittle autumn leaves.

The three men sighed.

"We climbed your
tallest pine, and the
wind rocked us
back and forth,"
said Mr. Oddic.
"It
still
does,"
said
Ms.
April.

"When we were boys, we used
to fly kites up here," said Mr. Iddy.
"It was the prettiest place
in the whole town."
"It still is,"
said Ms. April.

"We built dams in the pond and watched frogs, and dragonflies lit on our noses," said Mr. Dimm.

"They still do," said Ms. April. "Boys, you may always play here,

for I promised this field and forest,

pond and hill, would always be," said Ms. April.

"But Ms. April," said Mr. Iddy. "One, this empty land is wasted!"

"Two, you can't keep old promises," said Mr. Oddic. "Or stop progress."

"And three, you're too old to be left alone," said Mr. Dimm.

"Wasted land? Old promises? All alone?" said Ms. April as the parlor door opened.

"Boys, may I introduce . . .

my nieces
from back east,
and my cousins
from down south?"

"Here are my uncles from out west,
and my aunts from up north."

The room swelled with all shapes,
   all sizes,
      all colors of skin and hair.

They each had Ms. April's
   bright, bright eyes
and friendly smile, some with
sharp, sharp teeth.

"Look at the time!" said Misters Iddy, Oddic, and Dimm. "Thank you for the tea, but we must run!"

And run they did, down the hill, past the stone wall, followed by every bulldozer, dump truck, and back loader, all the way to town.

"Too many relatives," said Mr. Oddic, "with a definite family resemblance."

"Foxy old girl," said Mr. Dimm. "She was everywhere at once."

Mr. Iddy opened the window, wet his finger, and held it up to test the wind.

"Where," he asked, "did I put my old kite?"

"Ah," said Ms. April as she trotted, tip, tip, tap, up the attic stairs. "Peace at last."

She pulled off her gloves, unwrapped her veil,
and drew the pin from her best hat.
She kicked off her boots, slipped off her brocade jacket,
shimmied out of her old overalls,
and—surprise, surprise, Misters Iddy, Oddic, and Dimm—

it had not been Ms. April, but Ms. Mae, all along.

Ms. Mae shook out her elegant red tail and trotted, tip, tip, tap,
away from the dusty attic and into the sweet night air,
where fireflies flicked and tree frogs peeped,

and all her friends and relatives waited.

"Thank you, my dears," said Ms. Mae.
She kissed each one of them and watched them go,
    some to their warm beds, some to keep company
with the night.

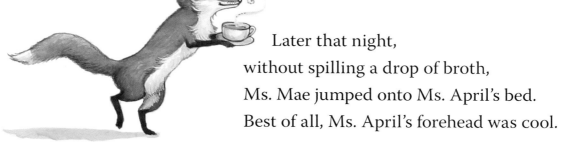

Later that night,
without spilling a drop of broth,
Ms. Mae jumped onto Ms. April's bed.
Best of all, Ms. April's forehead was cool.

"I just woke up," said Ms. April. "Did I miss anything?"

"Not a thing," said Ms. Mae. "Have some soup."

"Thank you, my dear," said Ms. April. "What would I do without you?"

"No, my dear," said Ms. Mae. "The question is, what would *we* do without *you*?"

Ms. Mae rested her sharp nose on her neat, black paws.
With one ear ready for the smallest sigh, Ms. Mae slept with a peaceful heart,
knowing their field and forest, pond and hill, would always be.

Ms. April Park

Karen Dugan is the artist or author/artist of twenty previous children's books, many of them prizewinners (Reading Rainbow selection winner; Skipping Stone Honor Award; winner, Scientific American Young Reader's Book Awards–Multicultural; winner, International Reading Association; Honor Notable Children's Book of the Year).

Explaining the genesis of *Ms. April & Ms. Mae*, Karen Dugan says, "I wanted to explore the kinship of all creatures and the imbalance we humans have created. I admire animals' perfection and ability to exist and survive without clothes, electronics, or money. We humans can't fly, or hibernate, or hear mice moving below the snow. We can't pollinate flowers, or spin silk from our abdomens, or weave nests with our mouths. Our hands are marvelous, and sometimes our brains, too. Though we have invented incredible, amazing things, we have also used these inventions for terrible cruelty, and therein lies the difference.

"We still have so much to learn and relearn, and I worry that we are canceling out the very beings who could teach us. We care for our elderly, but if I tell someone about two young crows feeding a crippled, half-blind old crow, that fact is not listened to with the same interest. We forget that we belong to that animal world, which means we are accountable for our treatment of our fellow creatures.

"In *Ms. April & Ms. Mae*, I ask a question: What if there were an animal who talked our talk, who walked between both worlds? What would an intelligent animal do if all her relatives and their homes were threatened? As human beings, what would we do if we were the ones whose numbers were being controlled, our homes destroyed? We'd call the police, go to court, or fight a war.

"*Ms. April & Ms. Mae* takes another path. In these pages I am talking about the possibility of civility to all, of walking as gently as possible upon this earth."